TREASURE ISLAND

BONNEY PRESS

Published by Bonney Press,
an imprint of Hinkler Books Pty Ltd
45–55 Fairchild Street
Heatherton Victoria 3202 Australia
www.hinkler.com

BONNEY
PRESS

© Hinkler Books Pty Ltd 2019

Cover design: Jess Matthews
Illustrator: George Ermos
Text adapted by: Katie Hewat
Design: Paul Scott and Patricia Hodges
Editorial: Emily Murray
Prepress: Splitting Image

ISBN: 978 1 4889 1303 7

Printed and bound in China

TREASURE ISLAND

Based on the original story by
ROBERT LOUIS STEVENSON

I'll never forget the night I first met the bloodthirsty pirate, Billy Bones. A great storm was blowing in from the sea and the wind was shaking the walls of the Admiral Benbow Inn, which my mother and I owned and ran. Thunder bellowed and lightning streaked the sky.

Then, between the rolls of thunder, I heard a man coming down the path singing an old pirate shanty:

'Fifteen men on a dead man's chest,

Yo-ho-ho and a bottle of rum!'

This was followed by a loud banging at the door, and I opened it to find that our visitor was a tall man with a vivid red scar across his left cheek. He wore a filthy blue coat and carried a cutlass, knife and pistol in his belt. He was dragging a heavy chest behind him, which he dropped on the floor as he entered the inn.

'I'm Billy Bones,' he declared grandly. 'No doubt you've heard of me?' I shook my head and he looked rather offended. 'Who are you, then?' he asked.

'Jim Hawkins,' I answered nervously.

'Well, Master Hawkins, do you get many visitors here?' he asked. When I told him that our inn was a quiet place, he seemed very pleased.

'Good!' he said. 'I'm not wanting to see any strangers ... or old friends for that matter,' he added darkly. I served him a quick meal and showed him to his room. He lugged his trunk up the stairs and slid it under the bed.

I locked up the inn and went to my own bed, hoping that Billy Bones would not stay for long.

But Billy stayed for a few weeks, and then a few weeks more. He was a terribly unpleasant guest and he drove our other customers away. Worst of all, he constantly carried his knife and his pistol. My mother was too afraid to ask him to leave, though he had not paid her a penny since he'd arrived.

One day, another man came looking for Billy Bones. This man had a patch over one eye, two missing fingers and a cutlass: he couldn't have looked more like a pirate if he'd bought a costume. Billy was out, so the man sat near the fire and waited. When Billy finally came back through the door, he let out a low hiss. 'Black Dog, you lily-livered scoundrel!' he snarled.

'If it isn't my old friend Billy Bones!' sneered Black Dog. 'I believe you have something that belongs to me and the crew.'

'You'll never get that map from me,' said Billy. With that, he launched himself across the room at Black Dog and a great struggle ensued. The two pirates kicked and hit and bit each other. They pulled at each other's hair and poked at each other's eyes – it was not at all like the valiant fights I had read about in my favourite pirate stories! Finally, Black Dog backed away.

'You turn over that map by ten o'clock tonight, or I'll be back with the rest of the crew!' he shouted as he ran out of the inn.

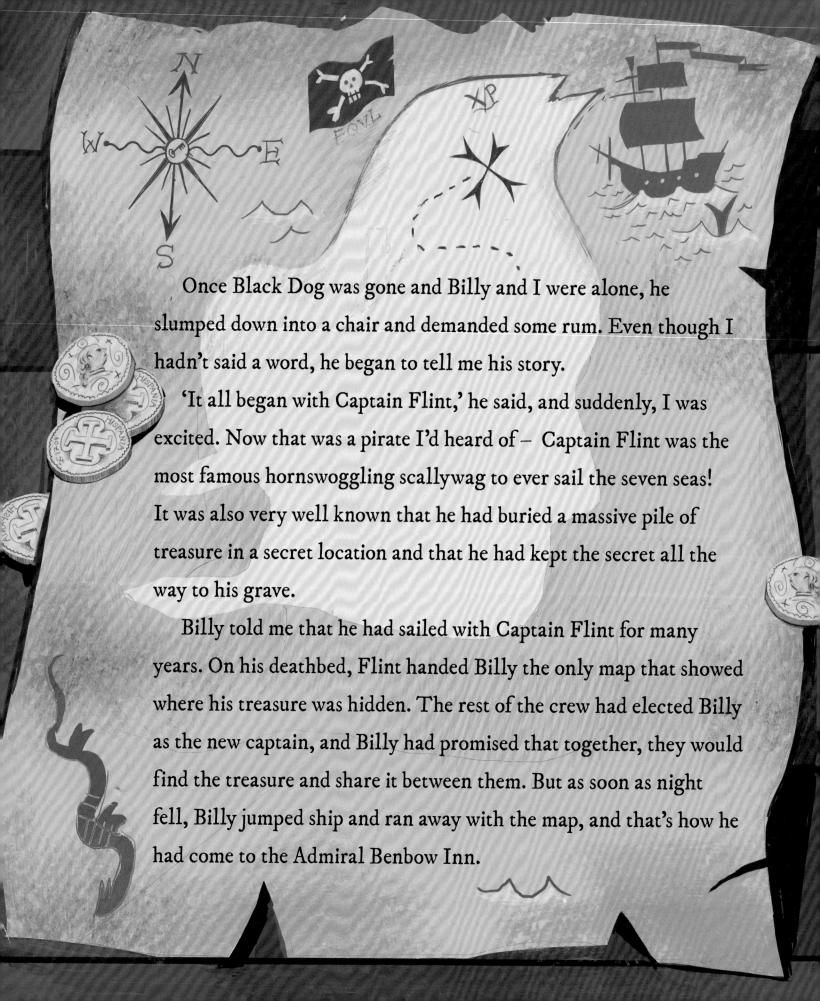

Once Black Dog was gone and Billy and I were alone, he slumped down into a chair and demanded some rum. Even though I hadn't said a word, he began to tell me his story.

'It all began with Captain Flint,' he said, and suddenly, I was excited. Now that was a pirate I'd heard of – Captain Flint was the most famous hornswoggling scallywag to ever sail the seven seas! It was also very well known that he had buried a massive pile of treasure in a secret location and that he had kept the secret all the way to his grave.

Billy told me that he had sailed with Captain Flint for many years. On his deathbed, Flint handed Billy the only map that showed where his treasure was hidden. The rest of the crew had elected Billy as the new captain, and Billy had promised that together, they would find the treasure and share it between them. But as soon as night fell, Billy jumped ship and ran away with the map, and that's how he had come to the Admiral Benbow Inn.

'Shiver me timbers, but there's only one thing for it,' said Billy, wringing his hands together. He was pale with worry. 'I'll have to weigh anchor and clear out of here before ten o'clock.' And with that, he jumped out of his seat and hurried up the stairs.

I must admit, I was glad that Billy was finally leaving, but I was also quite concerned about what would happen to my mother and me when this gang of cut-throat pirates arrived to find Billy gone and the map with him.

But I needn't have worried about any of that because, as Billy reached the top step, he suddenly turned, clutched at his chest, went as stiff as a statue, then tumbled all the way back down to the bottom of the stairs. He'd been so worried about getting caught that his heart had given out! And so Billy Bones was no more.

My mother, who had been watching and listening from the kitchen, came into the room. 'Well, come on, Jim!' she said to me. 'We'd better find this map.'

The two of us hurried upstairs to Billy's room and pried open the lock on his trunk with a knife. We sifted through everything until we finally found an old piece of parchment at the bottom. My whole body shivered with excitement as I read the heading:

TREASURE ISLAND.

Just then, the clock began to chime ten ... and between the chimes we heard footsteps outside. We hugged each other in fright.

'We've got to get out of here!' I whispered. I stuffed the map into my shirt, then dragged my mother downstairs, through the kitchen and out the back door. We went straight into town to the home of our friend, Dr. Livesey.

Dr. Livesey gave us hot tea and listened to our tale with growing excitement. 'A real treasure map!' he gasped when we showed him the parchment. 'And the famous Captain Flint's, by Jove! We must show this to Squire Trelawney as soon as possible – he'll know what to do.'

The following morning we set off to see the squire, who nearly fell off his chair when we showed him the map. And he sure did know what to do – he funded a treasure hunt!

Six weeks later, after much organisation and preparation, I was aboard a lovely ship called the *Hispaniola*. Also aboard were Dr. Livesey, Squire Trelawney and the rest of the crew that the squire had hired. I had been introduced to them all, but I had become closest to the galley cook – a man named Long John Silver.

Silver was rather an odd-looking fellow. He was missing one leg and had a carved wooden stick in its place. He also had a large green parrot that sat on his shoulder and squawked a lot of nonsense, but none of it really made sense to me. Some of its favourite sayings were 'Argh, me hearties', 'Ahoy, matey', and 'Walk the plank!'

Silver told me stories and taught me about life at sea. He always told me I was as 'smart as paint'. I wasn't sure how smart paint could really be, but we became good friends anyway.

So, one evening I was very surprised to hear Silver and another crew member, Israel Hands, talking quietly.

'When can we finally take over this ship?' asked Israel. 'The men are getting restless.'

'As soon as we get hold of the map,' replied Silver. 'Then we'll throw that landlubbing squire and his men overboard and find Flint's treasure!'

I couldn't believe my ears – Silver was a mutinous pirate! Who'd ever heard of a peg-legged pirate with a parrot on his shoulder? As they discussed their plan, I learned that most of the crew on board were Silver's own people.

I waited until Silver and Hands were gone, then I ran straight to the squire's cabin. I told him what I had overheard and he sent me to fetch the other men he knew to be loyal: Dr. Livesey, Captain Smollett and three others.

Together we discussed the dire situation. The squire spoke: 'We can't turn back towards home or the rotten rascals will mutiny. We must make it to the island before they find the map. Luckily, I have it hidden away where they'll never find it.' Captain Smollett nodded thoughtfully, and told us he had an idea.

A few days later, we reached the island and dropped anchor. The squire had been right – for all they had tried, the pirates had not been able to find the map. It was time to put the next part of our plan into action.

Silver and his crew were sent ashore to find fresh water and a place to camp, which they were happy to do after a long voyage. They still had no idea that we knew of their treachery, and they expected us to follow a few hours later once we had completed our chores on board.

Instead, as soon as darkness fell, we sailed the ship around to the other side of the island. We knew from the map that there was a small fort there, so we dropped the anchor, loaded as many supplies as we could onto two rowboats, and went ashore.

It wasn't until the next day that Silver realised what we had done and, when he finally found our hideout, he was very angry at having been fooled. We were ready and waiting for the pirates' arrival, knowing that we would have to defend ourselves against a group that was twice our number.

'We have you surrounded!' Silver shouted from the clearing outside the fort. 'But I shall leave you all unharmed if you just hand over the map.'

The squire shouted back his refusal and the first cracks of gunfire filled the air. Soon everybody was firing wildly, the air was thick with smoke and splinters of wood were flying everywhere. I did as I was instructed, and ran between each man in the fort, reloading one musket while he fired another.

Eventually the firing outside slowed down, and then stopped all together. I ran to the window and could see nobody outside. 'They've gone!' I shouted. 'We've won!'

But the captain just shook his head. 'They'll be back,' he said.

The next day came, but there was no sign of Silver. I was bored of being cooped up in the fort, so I offered to explore the island and spy on the pirate camp.

I headed out of the fort and across the island but, before I could find the pirates, I found something far more extraordinary on the hillside: a strange creature hopping from rock to rock. It moved as nimbly as a mountain goat, but it didn't look like any beast I had seen before. It finally stopped, turned and stared at me, and then I realised it was a man! He seemed nervous at first, then slowly started to climb closer and closer to where I stood. And then he spoke.

'Got any cheese?' he asked. It wasn't quite what I was expecting him to say, but I did have a piece of cheese wrapped in cloth in my pocket, which I had brought along for my lunch. I pulled it out and offered it to him, and he quickly reached across and snatched it. He took a bite, then he screwed up his face in happiness and leaped from one leg to the other. I waited until he had finished the cheese, then asked him who he was and what he was doing here.

'The name's Ben Gunn,' he said, 'and I haven't seen another human in three years.' Ben explained that he had been marooned on the island. I told him about my friends and the pirates and invited him back to the fort. He refused, but he did ask me to send the doctor out to see him, which I agreed to do.

Back at the fort, the others were very interested in Ben's story. They thought he might even know something helpful about the island or the treasure. Everyone agreed that the doctor should visit him the very next day.

The next morning, all was still quiet, so I decided to go out exploring again. I slipped quietly out of the fort before the others awoke and wandered along the beach, through the forest and up the hill.

I was having a grand old adventure, until I realised the sun was beginning to set and I was a long way from the fort. I made my way back as quickly as I could, but it was well after dark when I arrived. I was expecting a good telling off from Dr. Livesey, but when I opened the door to the inner hall, all I could hear was snoring.

Relieved, I crept through towards my sleeping mat, but in the dark I managed to trip over a sleeping body. At first I thought it was one of our men, but then out of the darkness I heard a squawk: 'Walk the plank!'

Voices yelled in the dark, and someone lit a lantern. I looked around in the dim light and realised that I had tripped over Long John Silver – and the fort was full of his men. There was no escape.

'Well, hello Jim Boy!' said Silver in that fake friendly way of his. 'I knew you'd come to your senses and join us. I've always thought you'd make a fine pirate!'

'What have you done with the others?' I demanded.

'Not to worry,' said Silver. 'We made a little deal earlier today. I got the map, and they got to leave with their lives.' He saw that I was puzzled and must have guessed that I was wondering why they had gone without me. Had they forgotten me?

Silver chuckled. 'No, my boy, they didn't forget you. When you disappeared, they thought you might have changed sides. I was happy to tell them that was true. Anyway, better get some rest. We're hunting for treasure tomorrow!'

We were up and ready to go early the following morning. Silver read the directions on the map aloud: Start Skeleton Island. Big tree. North-west to Spy Glass Hill. Tall tree. Ten paces south.

From the map, we could see that Skeleton Island was a tiny island that lay alongside the bigger island we were on. We made our way down to the shore and piled into two rowboats. When we reached Skeleton Island, Silver ordered the men to fan out and search for a big tree. He was worried that, given the chance, I would run off, so he brought a rope from the boat, which he tied through my belt to his own to stop me from getting away.

A short while later we heard a shout from within the forest. We rushed towards the sound and were horrified to find Israel Hands standing over a skeleton. It had an eye patch and a tatty blue jacket with a cutlass tucked into the belt. But most strangely of all, while one bony arm was resting by its side, the other was outstretched, as if pointing back to the main island. Silver pulled out his compass and placed it alongside the pointing arm.

'Praise the stars!' said Silver. 'This is one of Flint's jokes. He always was a black-hearted joker. If I'm not mistaken, these arm bones are pointing straight to the treasure.' Captain Flint had left a skeleton to show us the way.

So, we loaded into the boats and rowed back to Treasure Island. Once we were ashore, we headed towards Spyglass Hill in search of the big tree. I couldn't help but wonder what other surprises Captain Flint might have left for us.

Finally we reached a clump of trees, in the very centre of which stood an enormous tree that towered above the rest. Silver rubbed his hands together and did a little jig: well, a sort of jig given he had a peg for a leg. 'We're almost there! It's so close, I can smell the treasure!'

Flint stood at the base of the tree and held out his compass. 'Now for the final clue,' he said. 'Ten paces south.' With that, he began counting out the steps. At six he ordered the men to ready their shovels, at eight he was visibly quivering with excitement, but at ten he let out a great cry of anger. We stood at the edge of an enormous pit, and inside the pit was ... absolutely nothing.

Somebody had already found the treasure!

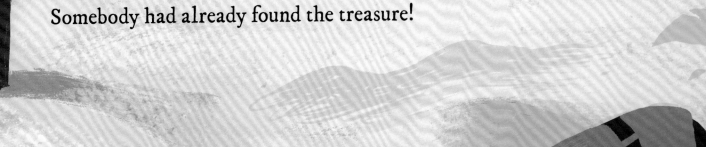

As we all stood in shocked silence, we heard a voice call out from the tree line. 'Stay where you are, you no-good stinking pirates!'

It was Squire Trelawney! He stepped out from the trees, along with Dr. Livesey, Captain Smollett and Ben Gunn. All the pirates except Silver, who still had me tied to him, bolted for the cover of the trees on the opposite side. The squire let off a musket shot but it went wide and they all got away.

The captain kept his musket aimed at Silver and the doctor rushed over to untie me. He gave me a fond pat on the head. 'I'm glad to see you safe and well, Jim!' he said. 'We never thought for a moment that you would join the pirates.' I couldn't begin to describe my relief!

The doctor told us what had happened while I was out exploring: 'I went to see Ben Gunn, and learned that he had dug up the treasure and hidden it somewhere else. That made the map useless, so I gave it to you, Silver. After all, you did say you wanted it. Then we set up this ambush and waited for you to come to us.'

Silver scowled, and the doctor seemed quite pleased with himself.

The next morning, Ben took us to the treasure, which he had hidden in a cave down by the beach. I don't think any of us were truly prepared for the huge fortune Captain Flint had collected: there were rows upon rows of gold bars, chests full of gold coins and others overflowing with jewels! While the rest of us were awed, Silver seemed distraught by the amount of treasure that could have been his. I could swear I even saw a tear slide from the corner of his eye and down his cheek.

We spent all that day loading the treasure onto rowboats and out to the *Hispaniola*. We had the treasure and we were going home!

Silver was to come with us. He would be taken back home and charged with piracy. We would leave the other pirates marooned on the island. Ben Gunn assured us that would be as harsh a punishment as any. We left them some food and supplies on the beach before we made our final trip out to board the ship and set sail. They would never cause trouble on the high seas again.

After a few weeks at sea, we pulled into a busy port for fresh water. We left Ben Gunn onboard to watch over Long John Silver and went ashore. When we climbed back aboard at the end of the day, I noticed that Silver was not in his usual spot on the deck. I asked Ben where he was and Ben, rather sheepishly, admitted he had let Silver escape.

We were all outraged at first, but then Ben explained: 'I could see him sitting there plotting, day after day. He would not have rested until he found a way to take the ship and steal the treasure. I gave him a bag of gold and sent him on his way before anyone was hurt.'

After everything Silver had done, we all supposed Ben was probably right, so we set off on the last leg of our extraordinary journey.

When we finally docked at our home port, all I could think about was seeing my mother! I picked up the heavy sack that contained my cut of the treasure and raced down the gangplank and up the street on wobbly legs that weren't used to being back on land.

I hired the first carriage I saw to take me to the Admiral Benbow Inn as fast as the horses could take us. When we finally reached the inn, I saw my mother sweeping the front doorstep. She stopped when she saw me and a smile lit up her face.

I ran to the front door and swept my mother into a hug, twirling her around and planting a giant kiss on her forehead. 'Did you miss me, Ma?' I asked, and she simply cried. But when I showed her what was in my sack, she began to laugh and I hugged her again. I was so very glad to be home, and decided I was more than happy to be a regular landlubber for the rest of my days.